My Fox Ate My Cake

David Blaze

For Zander...

Wow! That's Awesome!

Whatever!

CONTENTS

FRIDAY AFTERNOON

I stared across the rickety old table and into the eyes of my sworn enemy—Shane Connors. The school bully had grown another two inches taller and three times meaner than the first day I met him. I wanted to crawl under the table and hide forever.

It was my twelfth birthday party and my mom had invited half of the school to surprise me in my backyard. I was surprised alright. Shane had been standing in the middle of everyone, pounding his fists together and laughing at me. It was my fault he was there. I never told my mom about him and the homework assignment I wrote for him.

She had set the backyard up with tons of games she thought the kids would love, like Poop the Potato—where two kids raced with potatoes between their legs then 'pooped' the potatoes into buckets. Seriously? I wasn't exactly the coolest guy at school, but whatever reputation I had was destroyed with the word Poop.

I glanced across the yard at my house and through the

sliding glass door. All of the adults were inside doing whatever adults do. My mom looked back at me, smiled, and gave me two thumbs up. I love my mom and I'd do anything for her, but she had created my worst nightmare on my biggest day.

She had put together another table covered with every kind of candy you can imagine. She called it a candy buffet. Chocolate, licorice, mints, gummies ... everything! The candy was piled so high that it would take weeks to eat it all.

But there was one problem. One *major* problem.

My mom had decided whoever won each game would win a handful of candy. It sounded fair, but Shane won every game. He had a plastic bag full of candy he kept waving in front of our faces. Every other kid complained to me that they couldn't get any.

I flinched when Shane stretched his arm across the unsteady table. He rested his elbow on the table and raised his hand straight up. "You're going to lose, Jonah," he snickered. "You know why?" He flexed his arm and stared at his biceps. "Because that's what losers do, Jonah." I bit my lip because I didn't like being called that name and he knew it.

This was an arm-wrestling contest, and he had already beaten every other kid there. He was so big and strong that it was a joke to think anyone could win against him. I'd be lucky enough to walk away without a cast on my hand.

I looked around at all the kids surrounding us in a

circle. There were at least thirty of them. Most of them were on my side of the table. My mind screamed for one of them to take my place. My heart raced in fear. This didn't feel like a birthday party at all!

I took a deep breath and put my elbow next to Shane's on the table. I locked my hand with his and sat up straight. Maybe I could lessen the impact of my hand being crushed.

My cousin Dana leaned across the table and asked if we were ready. I nodded. She had light brown hair tied back in two ponytails and huge dimples when she smiled. But she seldom smiled. She was only seven years old and was always in charge of everything. Some people would call her bossy. I wondered how we could come from the same family. "Go!" she shouted.

I tightened my grip and pressed against Shane's hand as hard as I could. My only goal was to walk away without someone calling an ambulance for me.

But that didn't happen.

My hand didn't sway one way or the other. I looked back into Shane's eyes, confused. He was sweating and pushing as hard as he could. Was this really happening? I wouldn't have thought it in a million years, but I was as strong as him.

Dana looked at me and almost smiled. She shouted my name. "Joe!" I'm glad she didn't call me Jonah. I have my reasons for being called Joe. Dana turned to each side and shouted, "Joe! Joe! Joe! Joe!"

The other kids joined her and chanted in unison, "Joe! Joe! Joe! Joe!" I felt stronger every time they shouted my name. Shane's hand began to sink toward the table. This was really happening! I was going to beat him!

"You can do it, Joe," Melissa assured me from the side. She was pretty with her huge smile and long, brown ponytails. I remembered the first time I met her in school a few months ago. She gave me hope. I wasn't allowed to have a girlfriend yet, but if I was, I'd want it to be her. "I believe in you."

For the first time ever, I saw fear in Shane's eyes. I'll never forget how embarrassed he was after reading the paper I wrote for him at school. I had avoided him every day after that until now. I thought for sure he would beat me up.

Shane's hand was only inches from the table. I was about to win. Why had I been so afraid of him? I needed to be more like Dana. She was small and young, but she wasn't afraid of anyone. I smirked at Shane as I prepared to tap his hand on the table.

But that didn't happen.

Shane lurched forward. A sharp pain shot through my leg. Not the kind of pain that makes you want to find an aspirin. This was the kind of pain that made me want to scream like a fox!

I lost my concentration. Shane slammed my hand on the table then jumped out of his seat and threw his arms up in victory.

I fell out of my chair and grabbed my leg. It was swelling up like a basketball. The pain was unbearable. I panted so hard I could barely breathe. I wanted to vomit. I pointed at Shane. "You cheated."

Melissa kneeled next to me. "Are you okay?"

I shook my head. I took a few deep breaths and let my heartbeat slow down. "He kicked me," I complained. "I was going to win, and he kicked me."

Shane towered over me and laughed. It reminded me of the first day I met him. He had shoved me down and stood over me just like now. "You should've never messed with me," he barked. "Now you're going to pay."

Before I could respond, Dana jumped in front of Shane and pushed him back. He didn't move far because she was so much younger and smaller than him. "Back off, you big lug!" she shouted. "Leave him alone!"

Shane looked past her and down at me. He howled like this was the funniest thing he'd ever seen. "You can't even fight for yourself," he spit at me. "A little girl has to do it for you. How pathetic!"

One kid in the crowd chuckled. Everyone else stared with blank expressions. None of them were brave enough to stand up to this monster, but my little cousin was. I stood up slowly and balanced my weight on my good leg. I was as wobbly as the table we were just sitting at.

Dana turned to face me and held her palm out. "I've

got this," she said confidently. And I knew she did, so I nodded. I stood close because I wasn't going to let anything bad happen to her. "You know what else is pathetic?" she asked as she faced Shane again. He looked like a mountain in front of her. "It's pathetic when it takes a little girl like me to beat a big girl like you."

Everyone laughed and cheered for Dana. They pointed at Shane and said things like, "She called him a girl!" and "He's a big girl!" They hooted and hollered until Shane grabbed his bag of candy and marched right past me.

"You're dead meat," he promised me before he disappeared back into the house. I had no doubt he meant every word.

Dana grabbed my hand and held it up as high as she could. "Winner!" she declared. I knew she meant I was the winner of the arm-wrestling match, but I had won so much more. Everyone cheered for me.

I looked over at the huge table of candy, knowing I had won the next handful. It was too far for me to walk until the throbbing in my leg went away. "Melissa, get two handfuls of candy for me, please."

She gave me a confused, weird look. I could tell she was disappointed I was willing to break the rules. We were only allowed to take one handful when we won. "It's okay," I told her. "It's my party, so it's my candy."

She sighed before walking to the table and doing exactly what I asked. When she returned, she shoved her hands toward me full of candy. "Just take it," she said, shaking her head. "You're not the person I thought you were."

"I'm sorry," I replied, feeling like I had lost a friend. I pointed at all the kids around us. "But that candy's not for me. It's for everyone else." They had been complaining all afternoon that they couldn't get any candy because Shane kept winning it all. This was my way of making things right.

The kids rushed to Melissa and accepted the candy from her. She wouldn't stop smiling at me. I had a feeling we were still friends.

"Let's hear it for Joe!" Dana shouted, standing by my side and holding my arm up again. Everyone chanted with her like before. "Joe! Joe! Joe! Joe!"

It was a wonderful feeling, and I wish I could say the rest of the day was as awesome. But even after everything that had happened with Shane, it was all about to get ten times worse.

LATER FRIDAY

I tried my best not to smile when my mom and Uncle Mike walked into the backyard, holding a huge chocolate cake and singing "Happy Birthday". I was trying to look cool around my friends, but I was too excited to hide it. Officially twelve years old and one year away from being a teenager. Almost there!

My mom set the cake down on the same rickety table I had arm-wrestled Shane on. Where was he at? His dad, Mr. Connors, stood behind my mom and uncle with all the other parents. He had a smelly cigar in his mouth the last time I saw him. He tried to take this house away from us when we moved into it and my mom couldn't pay my late great-grandma's property taxes. I didn't trust him.

The other kids hovered over me and the cake. They were starving because the candy they got wasn't much at all.

"Make a wish, Jonah," my mom said. She was the only person allowed to call me that name. I only wanted one thing at that moment. I wished Fox was there to share this day with me. My stomach hurt just thinking about it. My best friend couldn't be there for his own protection.

After I blew the candles out, my uncle cut the cake and handed it on small plates to the kids. They devoured it right away and begged for more. I could only laugh.

"Why are you limping?" my mom asked.

I had forgotten about my bad leg. I didn't want her to know about Shane and worry about me. I also didn't want my uncle to hear that Dana challenged a guy ten times her size. My mom had done a lot to make this party happen and surprise me. I wasn't going to ruin it for her. "I banged it against that table," I told her, pointing at it.

"It's pretty bad," she said, sounding concerned. "Come inside when you're done, and we'll clean it up." I looked down at it. It was as red as an apple. "Before you do anything else, someone wants to wish you a happy birthday. He's pretty shy." She motioned for me to step away from the other kids.

I sighed and threw my hands up. We had been playing games in the backyard for what felt like hours and I could barely stand up. Now some kid wanted to wish me happy birthday? It had to be Shy Steve. That guy always sat by himself and avoided everyone.

I hobbled behind my mom past the outhouse and chicken coop. I remembered the first time I saw Fox there. I thought he was a dog—even with his brown hair that was almost orange, chest and tail that were white, and paws as black as night. I had fallen flat on my butt when he stood up on two legs and talked to me like a little kid. Ha!

My mom stopped by the back fence and faced me.
"What?" I asked her. "Why are we here?" I knew the
answer when I saw bright blue eyes peering through the
bushes.

It was Fox!

"I'll give you two a few minutes," my mom promised.
She smiled and headed back towards the party. We were
well out of view of everyone. This was the one gift I
wanted. I hadn't seen Fox in months. He had been
searching for something.

He leaped over the fence and stood in front of me on
his two hind legs. It amazed me how much he moved like a
human. I was worried because he wasn't smiling anymore
and had a serious look on his face. "If you dig a hole over
there," he said, pointing to the far end of the fence, "you'll

make it to China." He rubbed his chin and smirked. "And you know what they have in China?"

"Gold!" we both shouted at the same time. I couldn't stop smiling. He had tricked me once, but I researched it on the internet. You can't dig a hole to China.

"And why?" he continued.

"Because they have rainbows!" we said together. We both fell down laughing. My sides hurt as much from laughing as my bad leg hurt from Shane's kick. Fox kept rolling over and jumping up and down. I had missed this. I wished he could stay with me, but he was a wild animal. I was grateful for any time I could spend with him.

"I want to give you this," Fox said. I sat up when he handed me a wrapped present. "It's not much, and your mom helped."

It was awesome that he got me something for my birthday. He couldn't go into stores or even be seen in public. We agreed it was dangerous if other people found out what Fox could do. I opened the package to find a silver bracelet. "Thanks, Fox!"

"We're best friends, right?" he asked me. Of course we were. I couldn't imagine my life without him.

"We sure are," I promised him.

He wiped his forehead with a paw. "That's a good thing. Because otherwise I would look ridiculous in this." He had a bracelet just like mine beneath his paw. My mom had somehow fitted it for him.

I was grateful to have him in my life. I don't know how I ever lived without him. I couldn't explain our friendship to anyone else, but I never wanted to lose it.

I turned when a twig snapped behind me.

Shane was standing there with his cell phone pointed at us. It took a second for me to realize he had recorded Fox talking to me. My heart stopped. This couldn't be happening!

"I knew you were a freak. I've got you now," Shane threatened.

I faced Fox, pointed at the fence, and shouted, "Run!"

He leaped over the fence and disappeared back into the woods. I stared into the bushes and tried to figure out how to explain this to Shane. Surely he had a heart and wouldn't put Fox in any danger. I had to convince him to delete that video on his phone. I took a deep breath, prepared to beg my sworn enemy, and turned back to face him.

He was gone!

I watched him race past the outhouse and back into the crowd of kids and parents.

He was going to tell all the other kids and adults what he saw and then show them the proof. I ignored the pain in my leg and ran after him. I had no idea what he planned to do with that video, but it couldn't be good. I had embarrassed him more than once and he wanted to destroy me.

The backyard was crowded with kids and adults when I reached it—talking, laughing, pooping potatoes—none of them realizing my whole world was about to fall apart. I scanned through the crowd until I saw Shane next to the candy table by the back door.

He was with his dad, Mr. Connors. I couldn't breathe. Shane had his cell phone in front of his dad's face, playing the video he had recorded. They both looked up and stared at me.

I couldn't move. I was paralyzed.

Mr. Connors grabbed Shane and headed out of the yard. I couldn't let that happen.

"Stop!" I yelled. Everyone froze and stared at me. Then Mr. Connors did something I never expected.

He reached back to the candy table, grabbed two huge bowls full of candy, tossed the candy into the air and in front of me. "Candy for everyone!" he shouted.

The kids were scattered all over the backyard, but it only took a second for all of them to run in front of me and snatch the candy. They pushed and shoved. They were animals! And they completely blocked me!

I fought my way through the crowd, one kid at a time, desperate to get to Shane and his dad. Time was running out.

When I made it to the candy table, they were gone. The phone was gone. The video was gone. My hopes were gone. Tires squealed from the front yard. Shane and his dad were long gone.

"Is something wrong?" my mom asked, standing in front of me. "There's a lot more candy. And you have to eat some of your cake." She was the only person who could help me now. She had saved me more than once.

"Yep," my uncle Mike said, walking up to us with a plateful of cake in his hands. He had frosting all over his lips. "No one bakes a cake like your mom."

I tried my best not to cry, but I couldn't help it.

"Jonah," my mom said, "what's going on?" I could tell her because she knew about Fox. But I couldn't tell my uncle. He almost found out about Fox the same night my mom had, but we decided not to tell him. He was, after all, a hunter. The fewer people who knew we had a walking, talking fox the better.

"They know," I told my mom.

She gave me a confused look until I nodded at her. Then her eyes got big. "Who?"

I shook my head and balled my fists in anger. "Mr. Connors and his son." My stomach ached. "They recorded it."

Her eyes got even bigger. She searched through the crowd and realized Shane and his dad were gone. She cleared her throat and said, "Okay." She turned to my uncle. "We need to get everyone out of here. The party's over."

He stared at his plate and complained, "But I just started eating this cake." She grabbed him and turned him toward the kids and adults.

"Everyone, listen up!" my mom shouted into the crowd. "Thank you for coming today. I hope you had fun. We have a family emergency we need to handle. Please gather your things and leave as quickly as possible."

Some kids groaned. Their parents grabbed them and left one by one. My uncle Mike rushed them out, not even knowing why. I was amazed at his and my mom's ability to get everyone out so quickly, especially since there was so much candy and cake left behind.

Melissa grabbed my arm on her way out. "Is everything okay?"

I wished I could tell her the truth. Other than my mom, I trusted her more than anyone else. "I hope so."

"Alright now," my uncle Mike said, "keep it moving." He ushered her and her mom out of the yard.

Less than a few minutes later, the only people left in my backyard were me, my mom, my uncle, and my little cousin Dana. "Does this mean we get all the candy?" Dana asked.

My uncle Mike huffed. "No, it doesn't, young lady," he assured her. He looked back at my mom. "Does it?"

She was deep in thought and staring at the chicken coop. When she got like this, she couldn't hear anyone or even sense anything around her. She was formulating a plan.

My uncle grabbed her shoulders and shook her. "Sis? Mind telling me what just happened?" She was lost when she came out of her trance.

Then the one voice I didn't expect to hear interrupted everything.

"This doesn't taste like chicken," Fox complained, standing behind my uncle. He had cake all over his face and was trying to lick it off. Why was he revealing himself? I was worried about what was going to happen when my uncle turned around. No one could be prepared for what he was about to see.

"Look, kid," my uncle said, turning around, "the party's oooooooo… Oh, my gosh! Is that fox standing up and talking to me?"

Fox winked at me and raised his paws toward my uncle. "Chinese sneak attack!"

Dana stepped forward and yelled, "Awesome! A talking fox!"

I didn't know if my uncle would accept Fox. I didn't know what was going to happen with that video Shane recorded. All I knew was one thing—Fox was in danger, and I'd protect him as long as I could.

FRIDAY NIGHT

Fox agreed to stay inside with us until we figured out how to deal with Shane and his dad. We didn't know what to expect. I was happy to have my best friend in the house again because he had disappeared for so long. I hated it, but he said there was something he had to do—something he had to search for.

I had done a lot of research about foxes and learned what they liked to eat. They liked chickens! I couldn't believe Fox had tricked me so many times so he could get to the chicken coop. But we solved that problem. My mom kept chicken in the fridge and freezer so Fox could eat some any time he was there.

Fox and Dana were in my room with me that night. My mom sent us there so she and my uncle could talk about

Fox. They were brother and sister and loved each other, but there was a lot of yelling from the kitchen. I don't think my uncle approved of Fox at all.

Dana thought Fox was the most awesome thing ever. She kept petting him and talking to him like a baby. "Who's a good fox?" she said. "You are. Yes, you are!" Then she wrapped her arms around him and petted him. I don't think he was ever petted before, but he didn't have any problem with it. He rolled over on his back and let her rub his belly.

She lay down next to him and fell asleep within minutes. I put a blanket over her because I didn't know if my uncle planned to stay for the night. I guess she was exhausted from a long afternoon outside. We all were.

I yawned and stretched my arms out. "We should go to sleep," I told Fox. "I've got a feeling this is going to be a long weekend." I jumped on my bed. "You can sleep anywhere you want." I stood and took the top blanket off my bed, and laid it next to me on the floor. "This should be comfortable."

Fox shook his head. "I can't sleep here. This isn't anything like a den." He looked around the room like he was scared of it. I remembered the time I stayed in a hotel room with my mom. It was cool, but the bed didn't feel like mine, the room was freezing, the air conditioning made knocking sounds all night, and I could hear people talking outside. It was uncomfortable, and I didn't get any sleep.

"I have an idea," I said. I opened my closet and pulled

out three more blankets. Then I stepped out of my room and grabbed two chairs from the kitchen. I don't think my mom or uncle even noticed me because they were still arguing.

Back in my room, I set one chair on each side. I pulled my bookcase out of the corner and dragged it next to my bed. I grabbed a handful of pins out of the billboard on my wall.

"What's going on?" Fox asked, scratching his head.

"Watch the magic," I told him. I grabbed a blanket, stretched it out, and then laid one end across one chair and the other end across the other chair. I put the back of it on top of the bookcase. That made it look like a tent. It had gaps of air in some spaces because the blanket couldn't cover everything. I grabbed the other blankets and stretched them high across other areas of the room and pinned them to the walls as high as I could. Most of the room looked like a huge tent now. Maybe like a crazy person built it—but still like a tent.

"Welcome to my den," I said to Fox. I lifted one blanket end off the floor and revealed the room within it. Fox wagged his tail and stepped inside with me. It was dark, but I had grabbed a flashlight. I had learned to do all of this with my friend Tommy in the second grade. I had forgotten how much fun it was.

I turned the flashlight on and sat it straight up on the floor. It lit up the new den. "What do you think?" I asked Fox.

"It'll do." He gazed up at the blankets above us and smiled. He was happier here. I understood there were too many distractions in a room he had never slept in.

"This is fun," I said. "Hey—wanna hear a riddle?"

Fox threw his paws up. "What's a riddle?"

I guess he still had a lot to learn. I was glad he chose me to teach him. "It's like a joke."

"What's a joke?"

This was going to be harder than I thought. "A joke is like a funny story. A riddle is like a funny question."

He scratched his head.

"Okay," I said, "let's try one." I laughed before I even asked the question. I had read the riddle in a joke book years ago. "What has four wheels and flies?"

Fox rubbed his chin and stared at me. "I know the answer!" He smiled and said proudly, "It's a bird."

I shook my head. "Birds don't have wheels."

He blinked his eyes and pursed his lips. "What are wheels?"

I ran my hands through my hair. This was like trying to teach someone another language. "Cars and trucks have wheels. It's what makes them go." He still didn't understand. "Anyways, the answer is 'garbage truck.' A garbage truck has four wheels and it has flies—so it has four wheels and flies!" I tried to keep a straight face but couldn't stop laughing.

Fox looked at me like I was crazy. But he was a much faster learner than I thought. "I have a riddle. Wanna hear it?"

I made the mistake of saying, "Okay."

"Are you ready for this?" he asked. He laughed the same way I did before I asked my riddle. There was no way his could be better than mine. "What has four legs and farts?"

I tried to stop him, but it was too late. He let a fart rip

that was so loud and so long that all the blankets around us flapped like there was a tornado!

And then there was the smell. It was trapped in the den with us. It smelled like tuna and broccoli and onions and vinegar and dirty feet and dirty underwear all mixed together. It was disgusting.

"Whew," Fox said. "No more cake for me."

I couldn't breathe. I could taste the foul smell in my mouth. I pulled my shirt up over my nose and sucked in as little air as I could. I was worried I was going to pass out.

My bedroom door opened. I flicked the flashlight off so no one could see us.

"I'll get her," my uncle said. He was talking about Dana. "See you in the morning, Sis." His footsteps were louder on his way out.

"I wonder where Jonah and Fox could be," my mom said. "I don't see them anywhere."

I held a finger over my lips for Fox to keep quiet. This was a good den and I put a lot of work into it. No one would ever find us.

"What's that smell?" she asked. I knew exactly what it was. Fox's smelly fart. "Is that … is that sour cream and onion?"

Fox and I burst out laughing at the same time. Sour cream and onion! I hoped I never had to eat anything that tasted like that horrible smell around us.

"Is someone in there?" my mom asked. I guessed the jig was up. She knew someone was in the den, and it was our own fault.

I lifted up the blanket closest to her and stayed hidden behind it. I disguised my voice to sound like Darth Vader. "What's the password?"

She huffed and said, "I don't know the password, but I have a pizza that's half pepperoni and half chicken. Do you know anyone who wants some?"

I reached out and snatched the pizza tray from her. Before closing the den blanket, I accidentally said, "Thank you," in my real voice.

"That was close," I told Fox. "She almost saw us." I flicked the flashlight back on. Fox licked his lips when he saw the chicken on his half of the pizza. We both laughed and munched on our den meal. I loved pepperoni and Fox loved chicken. My mom was the best mom ever.

Fox burped when he was done. I have no idea how his little body held so much gas. I yawned and reached out of the den for my pillow and a blanket big enough to cover both of us.

"Where do you go, Fox?" I asked him as I lay down

and put part of the blanket over me. "When you don't come back for a long time." I had never asked him before, but I had a right to know the answer. I missed him when he was gone.

He was sitting down with his paws in front of him. He was silent for a moment, but he finally said, "Looking for my parents."

I never thought about Fox having parents, but of course he did. I sat up and asked him, "Where are they?"

The silence felt awkward. Fox's tail was limp by his side. I wished I had never asked the question and we could go back to laughing about farts.

"I was playing with my parents in the woods. Hide and Seek." He paused and smiled. "I was good at it. We would laugh and play and hug for hours." His smile disappeared, and his eyes focused on the floor.

"Two men with long guns came into the woods while

we were playing." He cleared his throat. "There was a loud bang, and the ground jumped up next to me. My parents yelled at me to run as fast as I could to the den. I did, and they were right behind me."

He fell silent again, and I didn't know if I should say something. I waited for him to continue.

"When we got there, they told me to go in first." He took a deep breath. "They said they loved me and were proud of me." He looked back at me. "Before I could stop them, they shoved me inside and buried me in with dirt and leaves."

I could tell he was hurting. Why did I have to ask him about this? I had no idea what happened to his parents or where they were. I couldn't imagine living with both of them gone. I was lucky to have my mom.

"I screamed for my parents to come inside. The den became so dark and quiet." He laid his head on the floor. "And then I heard two more loud bangs." He took another deep breath. "I scratched at the dirt and leaves to get out, but it took me days. Once I made it, I couldn't find my parents anywhere."

My heart hurt for Fox. I didn't know if he understood what happened, but I had a pretty good idea. I wasn't going to tell him.

He sat up again. "I wandered around for weeks, searching for food and water. And then I found this place." His tail wagged a little. "I found you."

I tried not to yawn. I had to say something to him. "I'm

sorry, Fox. No matter what happens, I will always protect you."

He stood up on all four paws. "Your mom's awesome. Where's your dad?"

I froze. I didn't expect that question to come up, and I wasn't prepared to answer it. I was afraid the other kids would think I was different. But this was my best friend. I was safe with him. He had just told me about the darkest moment in his life. Now I could tell him about mine.

I stared at my hands. "Two men in army uniforms came to our house in the city a few months ago." It was raining hard that day. I remembered my mom crying and screaming when they knocked on the door. "They said my dad wasn't coming back."

Fox put a paw on my hand. "We're more alike than I thought."

I nodded. "My mom lost her job soon after that, and we moved here. We left everything behind, but I'll never forget my dad. He taught me three things: Honesty, integrity, and compassion. He's the greatest man I've ever known. I hope I can be like him one day."

Fox laid his head on my leg and yawned. "He was a great man. What was his name?"

I wanted to make sure his name was never forgotten. "His name is Joe."

I lay back down and pulled the blanket over me and Fox. He cuddled up to my side. He felt warm and comfortable. We were both exhausted. I wasn't even sure if half of what I said made any sense. I flicked the flashlight off. "Fox?"

"Yes?"

"It still smells like sour cream and onion in here." I couldn't get the taste out of my mouth. It was disgusting.

"Nah," he said. "It smells more like farts." We both giggled.

I had one last thought before I closed my eyes and fell asleep. "I'm glad you're my best friend."

He yawned for the last time. "And I'm glad you're mine."

SATURDAY MORNING

My mom woke me up early in the morning and told me to get ready. She was crazy! First of all, how did she find me inside of that den? Second, I wasn't going anywhere without Fox.

"We're going to the farmers' market," my mom said. "Come on—the day won't wait for us forever." I was pretty sure the day would wait however long we needed it to.

"What about Fox?" I asked, pointing at him next to me. He was still asleep, and his tongue was sticking sideways out of his mouth. There was slobber everywhere.

"He'll be fine," my mom assured me. "Uncle Mike and Dana came back to watch him." She threw a T-shirt and a pair of jeans at me. "Get dressed." She walked out of the den and out of my room.

I slid the clothes on but didn't understand why we were doing this. Our number one priority had to be to protect Fox—not to sell rotten eggs at the farmers' market.

Fox woke up and wiped the slobber off his chin. "Where am I? And is there any chicken?"

I shook my head and told him about what my mom had planned. He didn't seem to care one way or the other. He kept talking about how his stomach was growling and he needed chicken. Barbecued chicken, baked chicken, fried chicken, chicken pot pie, chicken soup, chicken and rice—he wouldn't stop talking about it.

I led him into the kitchen. My mom and uncle were sitting at the table, drinking coffee. "Haven't seen the two chairs that are missing, have you?" my mom asked. Sure, they were in my room. I had to keep them as long as Fox was with us so we'd have a den.

"I have no idea what you're talking about," I told her. She winked at me.

Dana ran into the kitchen and threw her arms around Fox. "Good morning!" she shouted. I couldn't believe how happy she was to see him. It was weird to see her like that when she was always so bossy. "What do you want to do today?"

He looked around at everyone in the room. "Eat chicken." I laughed because that's all he ever wanted to do. Dana would get bored with him soon enough.

My uncle shook his head and grunted. "This isn't

right," he muttered. "It's not natural."

"Why can't we stay here?" I asked my mom. I didn't think it was safe to leave Fox with my uncle. He was a hunter and he didn't like Fox.

"We need to go," my mom said. "We don't want to draw any attention to ourselves. Everyone is expecting us to be there." She was right. We had made a lot of friends at the farmers' market and had a ton of loyal customers.

I didn't eat any breakfast because I felt sick leaving Fox at home. I gave Dana instructions for keeping him entertained. He loved watching cartoons after he realized they weren't real and they weren't after him. My uncle Mike stared at Fox—I wasn't sure *he* wouldn't be after him.

One of the last things I heard when I walked out the door with my mom was Dana saying, "We can have a tea party."

As expected, Fox replied, "I have a better idea. We can have a chicken party."

***

"There's our table," my mom said when we got to the farmers' market. Everyone knew it belonged to us because my mom reserved it every Saturday for the rest of the year. It was the same wooden table we started at months ago when we didn't know anyone in town.

"Good morning, ya'll," Mr. Jim Bob said in his strong country accent. His table was right next to ours and full of fruits and vegetables he had grown in his own backyard. I never saw him without that big straw hat on his head. I wondered what his hair looked like—or if he even had any left.

FARM GROWN

"Good morning to you, Jim Bob," my mom replied, helping me set the eggs from our chickens on our table. We still sold half a dozen eggs for six dollars. I never understood why we didn't just say they were one dollar each. "Can I interest you in some fresh eggs today?"

Mr. Jim Bob shook his head and said, "I appreciate the offer, ma'am, but there's no way in God's green earth I'd ever eat your eggs again." He stared at me when I chuckled.

My mom had convinced him months ago to buy two dozen eggs because the chickens were farm raised. He was a hard sell because he could have gotten them cheaper at the grocery store. He was grateful to get the fresh eggs that came from chickens my great-grandma Rita had raised. But we didn't know Old Nelly's eggs were packed in his cartons.

"I was sick for weeks!" he reminded us for the thousandth time. "I had to eat my food through a straw." He exaggerated, but there was some truth to it. Old Nelly was my great-grandma's favorite chicken, but she only laid rotten eggs.

I looked into the crowd all around the park. I was hoping to find Melissa, she came most Saturdays and we would hang out. Sometimes we would share one of those hamburgers they grilled there. I was disappointed when I didn't see her. Everyone was wearing jeans and T-shirts. The most popular material of the day was flannel. I thought it was strange when we first came here from the big city, but now here I was wearing jeans and a T-shirt like everyone else.

"What are you doing with those eggs?" someone said from the side of our table. I smiled because I knew who it was. Mr. Hunter stepped over to me, smiled, and shook my hand. "Good to see you, Joe." He nodded at my mom. I wondered how he had that long, gray mustache and bushy eyebrows but no hair on his head.

"Leave him alone," Mrs. Hunter said when she passed him and hugged my mom. She used to have some brown in her hair, but it had turned completely gray. "He's got better things to do than talk to an old geezer like you."

He put his hands on his hips like he was offended. "Women," he said, shaking his head. "Can't live with them—can't live without them."

"Oh, you hush," she said, giggling like a teenage girl. They were very much in love. She pulled my mom aside and said they needed a minute to catch up.

"So," Mr. Hunter said to me, "have you seen the gas prices lately? Almost three dollars a gallon!" I had no idea if that was good or bad, but I quickly calculated. I got a weekly allowance for doing my chores, and it was enough to get two gallons at that price. It took a lot more than that when I filled the gas tank for my mom.

"It's better than the old days," he continued. "I had to walk ten miles through the snow and sandspurs just to get to school." I doubted that was true because sandspurs can't grow in the snow. I nodded at him like I was amazed and believed everything he said.

"Jonathan," Mrs. Hunter said to him when she came back to us, "leave that boy alone. Quit trying to turn him into an old geezer like yourself." I tried not to laugh. She hooked an arm around his arm. "Let the kid enjoy his childhood while he can." She winked at me and pulled him away.

Mr. Hunter threw his hands up. "Sorry, Joe. Don't forget what I said about women."

I wanted to answer him, but I realized several kids were staring at me. Another pointed at me. I had no idea what their problem was. I moved my tongue around my teeth to make sure there wasn't something stuck in them. I didn't find anything. I looked down at my zipper to make sure it was up—all good.

Melissa caught me off guard when she appeared right in front of me. "Why didn't you tell me?" she asked. She wasn't smiling, and I had no idea what she was talking about. I could only stare at her, confused.

She pulled a cell phone out of her pocket, pushed a button on it, then shoved it in front of my face. I was shocked and wanted to tell her to be careful, but I couldn't. I saw the one thing I didn't expect to see.

A video of Fox talking to me was playing on her phone. It was the same one Shane had recorded. My heart was beating fast. "Where did you get this?"

She put the phone back in her pocket. "It's all over the internet. It already has over two million views." The twang in her voice got higher. "What's going on, Joe?"

All I could do was shrug my shoulders—even with all of the evidence in front of me. I don't sweat much, but my shirt was soaking wet. Melissa was the one person I had wanted to tell about Fox. Now that was taken away from me. Now the whole world knew about him.

"Let me see that again," I said to her. I was scared to death about what would happen to Fox. I couldn't even think straight because my head felt like it was about to explode. I grabbed the phone from Melissa and asked her to give me a minute. I had to show my mom. She agreed.

My mom was with another customer when I reached her. "Happy chickens make better tasting eggs," she told the man looking at the cartons.

She told me to hold on for a minute when I tried to get her attention. She was busy, but there wasn't any time to waste. I yelled her name. "Mom!"

She gave me an ugly face that let me know I was in big trouble. "I'll be right back," she told the customer. She grabbed me and pulled me aside. "Don't ever yell at me again. What's gotten into you?"

I put the phone in front of her face and let the video play, the same way Melissa had. My mom froze. I didn't think she was even breathing. "Mom? What are we gonna do?"

She snapped out of her trance and told me to get into the car because we needed to go home right away. I didn't argue. I grabbed the phone from her and gave it back to Melissa. "I'm sorry," I told her. "I'll explain everything later."

"What about my eggs?" the customer my mom had been with asked.

"Take them," she said. "You can pay me when you buy more next week."

SATURDAY AFTERNOON

My mom drove through town like a race car driver. She sped through every light. The tires squealed with every turn. I held on to my seat as tight as I could.

I ran to the house when we got there, not knowing what to expect. Uncle Mike didn't answer his cell phone when my mom called him from the farmers' market. I feared the worst. Maybe someone had seen the video and broken into our house. Maybe they had kidnapped Fox!

I threw the door open and nearly fainted.

Fox was sitting on the couch with my uncle, watching wrestling on TV. They were laughing and high fiving each other. I had thought for sure my uncle Mike would never accept him. "That's gonna hurt!" Fox shouted at the TV.

"Get a real job!" my uncle joined in.

My mom sighed and shook her head. "Boys will be boys." She walked over to the couch, tapped my uncle on the shoulder, and told him they needed to talk. He told her that he was busy bonding with his new friend and the wrestling match would be over soon.

She grabbed the remote control from him and

turned the TV off. "Mr. Awesome Muscles was about to make his move!" Fox whined. "The world needs his awesomeness!"

My mom huffed and said to my uncle, "You ruined him."

Fox stood up on the couch and flexed his hairy arms. "My name is Mr. Awesome Muscles. Prepare to feel my awesomeness!"

I couldn't stop laughing. Fox didn't have a single muscle on his body. I was surprised he didn't run from the big men fighting in their underwear on TV. I remembered when he was scared of cartoons and hid behind the couch.

"Calm down, Mr. Awesome Muscles," my mom said, trying not to laugh. She took out her cell phone and held it up for Fox and my uncle to see. She had found the video of Fox and was playing it.

My uncle stood up and said, "We have to do something." He looked at Fox like he was worried for him.

"I couldn't agree more," my mom said, turning to me. "Jonah, take Fox and Dana out back to feed the chickens. The grownups need to talk."

"But, Mom…" I said. I needed to be a part of whatever they were planning. I knew more about Fox than anyone else. And I had promised to protect him.

She came to me and put a hand on my shoulder.

"Let us talk for a minute, Jonah," she said softly so only I could hear. "We have to figure out what's best for Fox." She nodded slowly to make sure I understood. "We need to review all of our options, and we don't want to scare him. He's fragile."

Fox yelled from the couch, "My name is Mr. Awesome Muscles, and I'm going to bring the pain!"

"Maybe not too fragile," my mom said, patting my shoulder. I realized she wanted Fox out of the house so he didn't hear anything discussed that might scare him. And she wanted to make sure I could protect him.

"Come on, Fox," I said. "Let's go outside and play. You've been cooped up in here since yesterday." My mom smiled at me.

Dana walked into the living room from the kitchen with a tray of chicken nuggets in her hands. "What did I miss?"

I stepped outside with Dana and Fox and wondered what was going to happen next. I feared my best friend was in terrible danger.

"I'm not cleaning this up," Dana said with her arms crossed. "Your party, your mess—you do it." I didn't know what she meant at first and why she was so feisty, but when I looked at the backyard I realized it was a mess from my birthday party the day before.

"Is there any more cake?" Fox asked. I ignored

him because, after that nasty fart last night, I'd never let him eat cake again.

I looked at both of them like they were nuts. I held up the bag of chicken feed I brought with me. "We're just going to feed the chickens."

"Oh," Dana said, snatching the bag from me. "You should have said something sooner." She walked past us and kicked a balloon floating over the grass.

"You know what we should do?" Fox asked, rubbing his paws together. "We should find out what's inside that outhouse once and for all." He had a mischievous grin on his face that made me think he was up to something.

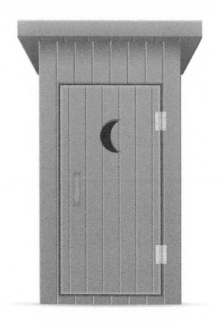

"You're not trying to trick me again—are you, Fox?" He had distracted me in the past so he could get to the chickens. I thought we had solved that problem, but old habits are hard to break.

"You have my word," he promised. "You know you wanna do it. I'll cover for you."

Dana came back to us. "What's taking you guys so long?" Her eyes were bulging out of her head like she was angry at us. "I'm not feeding those chickens by myself." She shoved the bag of feed back into my hands. "You do it."

"He wants to see what's in the outhouse," Fox told her. "But he's a scaredy-cat." I assured him that wasn't true. My mom wouldn't let me use the outhouse, and that made me want to see what was inside more than anything else.

"So you're a chicken?" Dana taunted me. "I get it. Everyone's scared of something." She nodded her head. "You're scared of an outhouse." She tucked her arms in and flapped them like wings. "Chicken. Bawk, bawk."

Fox licked his lips. "Mm, chicken."

I wasn't a chicken and told them as much. It was awesome to have a toilet outside. "I'll go in if you promise not to tell." They both nodded. Fox was standing with both front paws behind his back. I wasn't sure if he had a way to cross his fingers, but I was worried he did.

"Go on, chicken," Dana said, laughing. "Show us what you're made of."

I set the bag of feed down and marched to the outhouse. It was a wooden tower with a half-moon carved into it. I read on the internet that the moon had two purposes. In the old days, the half-moon meant it was for women. A star on the door meant it was for men. The main reason it was there was to let light in.

I took a deep breath and reached for the lock to open the outhouse door. I almost changed my mind because my mom told me to stay away from it. Maybe there was something inside I wasn't supposed to see. Maybe it was dangerous.

"Chicken!" Dana shouted. "Bawk, bawk, bawk, bawk." I turned to see Fox had joined her in flapping his arms and strutting around in circles.

I yanked the door open to show them I wasn't afraid. They'd have to eat their words.

Something green jumped out and attacked me! I ran from the outhouse as fast as I could, screaming for help.

Fox and Dana fell on the ground, laughing. They didn't care about me. My life was in danger, and all they could do was laugh.

"What's all that ruckus?" my mom asked, sticking her head out the back door. "I told you kids to feed the chickens."

"Joe's scared of a grasshopper," Dana said, laughing at my expense. "It jumped on him, and he can't stop screaming."

Fox nodded his head. "Look, I'm a chicken." He stood back up on his hind legs and flapped his arms.

My mom rubbed her temples. "Quit playing around. Go feed the chickens." She disappeared back inside, shaking her head.

The grasshopper jumped off of me and I was fine once I could breathe again. To be fair, I had no idea it was a grasshopper. All I knew was I was attacked. I should've listened to my mom and stayed out of the outhouse.

Dana and Fox joined me at the chicken coop. "Told you I wasn't a chicken," I informed them. They laughed at me.

"Mr. Awesome Muscles wouldn't have run," Fox said. "No sir."

I was glad no one else had seen what happened. And I hoped they never found out. Being in the sixth grade was hard enough already. "Just feed the chickens."

We grabbed handfuls of feed and threw it out to them as they wandered the fenced in area around the coop. Fox kept licking his lips.

As I watched the chickens eat, I realized Old Nelly wasn't outside. I didn't think Fox had anything to do with it, but I had to find out where she was.

"I'll be back in a minute," I told Fox and Dana. "I need to check on Old Nelly."

Fox took a step back. "Good luck. She likes to throw those rotten eggs. Don't come back smelling like farts." It was a risk I would have to take.

I stepped into the chicken coop and looked for her. I looked high. I looked low. I found her perched in the back, eyes closed, breathing heavily. Something was wrong.

I had no idea what to do. I had to tell my mom. Did they have a doctor for chickens? I hoped so because this was my great-grandma's favorite chicken and the last piece of her we had left. It was funny she thought Old Nelly laid golden eggs.

I turned to head out of the chicken coop to see if my mom was ready for us to come back into the house yet. I hoped they had good news for what we planned to do with Fox. I'd do whatever they wanted to keep him safe.

"Wait," some woman said from the back of the chicken coop. My heart jumped. I swear there wasn't anyone in there with me. I turned back to see Old Nelly stepping off of her rotten eggs. Her eyes popped open. "Please wait."

If that had happened a few months ago, I would have run out of there screaming for my life. I should have believed it when my great-grandma said Old Nelly talked to her.

"You have her eyes," Old Nelly said. I didn't know who she was talking about. I walked back to the old chicken. I kept my distance in case she wanted to throw one of her smelly eggs at me.

"Whose eyes?" I asked her.

Her breathing was hard, and she had a difficult time speaking. "Rita's. You have Rita's eyes." That was my great-grandma. My mom always said I favored her.

"Do you need help?" I asked her.

She tried to laugh. "I'm not a spring chicken anymore. My time is near." I think she smiled at me, but it was hard to tell because I'd never seen a chicken smile. "Rita made this a wonderful life for me. I enjoyed our conversations."

I wanted to know more about my great-grandma, but Old Nelly was speaking slower and slower. I had one question I needed to know the answer to.

"How did you and Fox learn to talk?"

Her eyes were half closed like she couldn't keep them open. I was afraid I would never hear the answer.

"This place is magical," she said painfully. "I was chosen to be here." She took a deep breath. "So was the fox." The next thing she said left me with more questions than answers.

"So were you, Joe." She closed her eyes and didn't move again or say anything else. How did she know my name? How did she live so long? What did she mean I was chosen? Chosen for what?

I stepped out of the chicken coop and let the sun hit my face. I was so confused I couldn't sense anything else around me. I only knew Old Nelly for a few minutes, but I would never forget her and what she said.

"Kids!" my mom shouted from the back porch. "Come back inside!" A few seconds after that she shouted, "Was someone in the outhouse?"

I had no intention of answering that question. I joined Fox and Dana as we headed back to the house.

Fox sniffed my pants and said, "At least you

don't smell any worse than you did before you went in there."

"Gee, thanks," was all I could say.

When we got back into the house, my mom had us sit on the couch in the living room. Fox had left some hairs behind on it. I picked them off, one at a time.

My mom and uncle stood in front of us. "We all know Fox was recorded talking in a video," my mom said. "That video has been seen by more than three million people now."

Dana faced Fox and put out a hand for a high five. "You're famous!"

My uncle said, "That's not a good thing. There's no other animal like Fox." He directed his attention to my best friend. "We don't know what this means for your future. You're going to receive a lot of attention."

Fox wasn't smiling. "I want to go home."

My mom sighed. "I don't think that's a good idea, Fox. People will be looking for you. Good people and bad people."

I could tell he was confused, and I knew he wanted to find his parents. "We'll take care of you. I'm sure we'll figure something out."

My mom agreed. "We need some time for this to blow over. We've already taken the first step."

I looked up at her. "What did you do?"

"I got in touch with Mr. Connors," my uncle said. "He assured me that he didn't know the video was online and he would never have allowed it. He's had his son take the video down." My mom showed us her phone. The link for the video was no longer available.

"This is good—right?" Fox asked.

"Yes," my mom agreed. "Mr. Connors wants to apologize for his son's behavior. I've invited them over for dinner tonight. We want to keep the peace."

I couldn't move. Shane was coming back here? In my house? I didn't trust him, and no matter what he said or did, I knew he had a mission to destroy me. Everyone around me was happy and relieved this was being resolved. I feared the real problem was only beginning.

SATURDAY NIGHT

I couldn't stop shaking as I helped my mom set the dinner table. I had goose bumps all over my arms like I did on my first day of school here in the country. I dropped a glass and it shattered on the floor. I was glad Fox didn't see any of that. I didn't want him to sense my fear. We had hidden him in the one place we didn't think anyone would look for a fox.

If I was rich, I would take Fox to Japan. I read about a village there where hundreds of foxes roam freely. You can run and play with them. Then he wouldn't have to worry about any of this and he could live with his own kind.

"Everything's going to work out," my mom promised. She grabbed a broom and dustpan.

I wanted to believe her, and I hoped she was right. I should have told her about Shane and how he bullied me, but there was too much going on. I didn't need her to worry about anything else at the moment.

I jumped when the doorbell rang. My sworn enemy was on the other side of the door with his dad. I wanted to leave the door locked and tell them to go away. But, instead, my mom told me to do the one thing that terrified me the most.

"Go let them in," she said. "I'll clean up this mess and get dinner on the table." I wanted to tell her that she could answer the door and I'd do everything else, but I didn't want her to know how nervous I was. I hoped I could get my uncle or Dana to do it, but they were at the dining table with their faces buried in their cell phones.

I took a deep breath, rolled my shoulders back, and headed for the front door. It wouldn't be that bad. They had already taken the video down. They wanted to make this right. Everything would be okay, like my mom said.

I opened the door and stared at the same face I had seen right there months ago. Mr. Connors was wearing the same striped suit he had on when he tried to take this house away from us for the IRS. The only thing missing was his smelly cigar. He was so big that I didn't see Shane behind him.

"Good evening, Joe," Mr. Connors said. "May we come in?"

Against my better judgment, I opened the door wide and let them in. It's not like I had a choice.

My uncle greeted Mr. Connors and led him to the dining table. Shane stepped in behind him and bent over to put his smug face in front of mine.

"You're dead meat, Jonah." He needed to come up with some new lines. Even though I had expected it, I swallowed hard.

"My name is Joe," I reminded him, slamming
the door shut and almost catching his fingers in it.
Maybe that would make him back off for the rest of
the night.

My mom called everyone to the dining table
because dinner was about to be served. Mr. Connors
grabbed her hand and said, "I'm sincerely sorry for
my son's behavior. That video should never have
happened." I didn't like the way he was holding her
hand. She slipped it away from him.

"But they're friends," he continued. He
redirected his attention to me. "And the boys were
just having fun—right, Joe?"

I wasn't sure how to respond. Shane was
definitely not my friend. And I never had fun with
him. He had probably lied to his dad to save his

hide.

Something didn't feel right. Mr. Connors didn't ask about Fox. He didn't even ask where Fox was.

The back door barreled open and slammed against the wall. I jumped. I had no idea who or what it was. But I saw the one thing that made my spine shiver. Shane and his dad were smiling.

A chubby man with a huge forehead and a hotdog nose walked right up to the dining table like it was his own house. He wouldn't stop laughing. "I got him, folks!" he shouted in the strongest country accent I'd ever heard. "No need to worry—I've got everything under control!"

Har!
Har!
Har!

My mom ran over and grabbed me. We both knew what he was talking about. But how? We had hidden Fox in the chicken coop. No logical person would look for him there.

"Who are you?" my uncle asked, standing up and challenging him. "What gives you the right to barge into this house?"

The man kept laughing. His tongue wouldn't stay inside of his mouth. "You don't know who I am? They know me around these parts!" He posed like he was a superhero about to get a picture. "I'm Tater the Exterminator!"

He held up a cage that he had been holding by his side. Fox whimpered inside of it. Tater shook the cage and beat a fist against it. "Quiet down, you filthy animal!"

I saw Fox's blue eyes through the slits in the cage. He was in there—trapped, scared, alone. "It's Fox," I told my mom. "He's got Fox!"

Tater stared at me with empty eyes and laughed. "No need to shout, young man. Like I said, I've got everything under control." He shook the cage again. "This little guy ain't gonna bother anyone else. Guaranteed!"

My mom let go of me and stepped closer to the crazy man. "You can't take him," she insisted. "That fox is our pet, and he's not a danger to anyone."

Tater the Exterminator laughed at her and said that was impossible. "It's illegal to own a fox in the great state of Alabama!" He lowered his voice for the first time. "You seem like law abiding citizens who don't want any trouble." He shook his head like he was concerned. "I'd hate to report you to the police."

My mom glanced back at me like she was exhausted and shrugged. I couldn't accept that. This man couldn't leave our house with Fox.

"Mom, do something," I begged her.

Mr. Connors stood up from the table with Shane by his side. "I'm sure it's all just a big misunderstanding. I'll do whatever I can to fight this." I didn't believe him. Shane wanted to destroy me, and his dad was helping him do it.

"Don't worry, little guy," Tater the Exterminator said to me as he passed by with Fox in the cage. "This critter's gonna be relocated somewhere far away, where he can't bother anyone else." My mom grabbed me again and held me tight.

Shane and his dad followed Tater the Exterminator as they headed for the door. I knew they were all together. What were they going to do with Fox?

"Stop!" I shouted. My mom held me tighter as I tried to break free. "You can't take him!" My uncle Mike and Dana stood on either side of me.

"We'll get him back," my mom promised. "Whatever we have to do."

"I'll make some calls," my uncle assured me.

Shane turned and smiled at me. "I told you not to mess with me," he gloated. With that, he walked out the door with his father, Tater the Exterminator, and my best friend—Fox.

"No!" I shouted. I couldn't stop crying.

Shane slammed the door shut behind them.

"Come back!" I screamed. "Please come back!"

SUNDAY MORNING

I sat in the church pew farthest in the back, hoping no one would see me. My mom called people who sat there Back Row Baptists. They could call me whatever they wanted to that day—I didn't get any sleep the night before because I couldn't stop worrying about Fox.

My plan didn't work because every kid in church crowded around me. They wouldn't stop asking me questions about the video with Fox. They thought I was the coolest kid ever, but I didn't care. Being cool didn't matter if Fox was in danger.

"Back away from him!" Dana shouted from behind me. Her voice traveled through the whole church. Everyone turned around and stared at me. I wanted to sink to the floor.

Dana stepped into my row and told everyone to

move their legs as she worked her way to me. I was in the middle. I was too tired to be embarrassed, so I closed my eyes and ignored everything around me.

"Take a hike," Dana said to whatever kid was next to me. There wasn't any argument and I felt her arms slide in by mine. Things got quieter. I hated to admit it, but I was glad I had a little bodyguard.

"Hey, Melissa!" she shouted. "Sit here!" I opened my eyes and looked around. Melissa always sat with her family, so I didn't expect that to change. Kids grunted as Melissa made her way through the row towards me on my other side.

Dana leaned across me and said to the girl next to me with too much makeup and a short dress on, "Hey, Blondie. You need Jesus. Go sit closer to the front." I couldn't move. Everyone was staring at me again and shaking their heads.

The girl stood up and said, "As if!" She shoved other kids' legs out of her way as she struggled to get out of the row when Melissa took her place.

Melissa was beautiful in her blue dress with colored polka dots. I wished I was brave enough to tell her that. She wouldn't look at me. She stared at the Bibles and hymnals shelved on the back of the pew in front of us. "Why didn't you tell me about the fox?"

I wasn't sure how to answer her. She seemed disappointed I had hid Fox from her. We were friends, but I didn't expect her to be hurt. "I didn't want you to think I was weird," I said.

She looked over at me and smiled. "Of course you're weird. Just be honest with me."

The church organ came to life and filled the sanctuary with music. I wondered if the organist knew more than one song. She played the same thing every Sunday.

"Brothers and sisters," the preacher said to all of us. I didn't catch much after that. The back row was warm and the lights were dim. I understood why so many adults sat back there. It was the perfect place to close your eyes and go to sleep.

I didn't plan to do that, but my head fell forward every few seconds. I realized I was falling asleep and kept jerking my head back. But, sure enough, my head wouldn't stay still. There was nothing I could do about it. The pew was comfortable, and I was exhausted.

Then the preacher said the one thing that made me open my eyes and sit up straight.

"The wolf also shall dwell with the lamb, and the leopard shall lie down with the kid; and the calf and the young lion and the fatling together; and a little child shall lead them."

I rubbed my eyes and tried to process what he said. There was a question I had to ask him when the service was over. It became more important to me than anything else.

It was time to leave when the organist played the same song again. I jumped up and tried to avoid the kids crowding me. Was that how it was going to be for the rest of my life? I hoped not. "I need to get out of here," I told Dana. "I've got to talk to the preacher."

She nodded like she was accepting a mission. "Out of the way, heathens!" she yelled at the kids. "Move it, move it!" I wasn't surprised when they cleared the row.

I weaved my way through the old people and young people and regular members I saw every Sunday. After I got through the foyer, I stood in front of the preacher. He wore a black suit with a red tie.

"I need to ask you something," I said to him.

He put a hand on my shoulder. "Of course, Joe. Go ahead."

I felt silly asking it, but I had to know the answer. "Do foxes go to heaven?"

He smiled and squeezed my shoulder. "I like to think so. God created all of us. He created foxes, giraffes, hamsters and elephants—every living creature. I hate to think of a world without them." He let go of my shoulder and bent down to my height. "It's important to love our animals as much as we can while they're here."

An old guy stepped up behind me and grabbed the pastor's hand. "Good sermon, brother. We need to talk about the budget."

I stepped out of the way and thought about what he said. I didn't want to think anything bad happened to Fox. I hoped he wasn't alone in some swamp or forest he had never seen. He was just a kid, like me. I was scared for him.

"What's going on, Joe?" Melissa asked when she stood by my side. "Be honest with me." I trusted her more than anyone else. I told her everything I knew about Fox, from the first day I met him.

She stopped me before I could finish. "Where is he now?"

I wished I knew the answer. I told her how Shane and his dad tricked my family. "Some guy named Tater the Exterminator took him. I don't know what to do. I have no idea how to find him." I searched for Tater the Exterminator on the internet, but he didn't have a webpage.

Mr. and Mrs. Hunter stopped next to me. "Hey, Joe," Mrs. Hunter said. "You're looking for Tater? He lives on Brown Street with his mom." She pointed to my right. "Big orange house—can't miss it. It's less than five minutes from here." She sprayed some perfume on her neck. It smelled like an old person.

I couldn't believe my luck. I knew where Tater the Exterminator lived. Maybe Fox was there!

"Tater is a disturbed young man," Mr. Hunter added. "A lot of loose screws."

Dana joined us and sniffed the air. "What stinks?"

"I've been meaning to pay Tater's mom a visit," Mrs. Hunter continued. "She's a lovely lady who's always left at home." She shook her head like she was angry. "Tater goes fishing on Sundays. He won't be back for hours." She snapped her fingers at her husband. "We should stop by and check on her."

He sighed and said, "Yes, dear." He rolled his eyes.

Melissa stared at me and nodded. I knew she was thinking the same thing as me. Maybe I could read other people's minds.

"You live across the street from us," Mrs. Hunter said to me. I realized that a few months ago when I knocked on their door and sold them all my chocolate. "You kids can catch a ride with us to Tater's house, and we'll drop you off at home—if your parents let you."

Dana pushed me forward and said, "What are

we waiting for?"

SUNDAY AFTERNOON

I knew Tater's mom was as weird as him when we were all sitting around a hot fireplace, sipping hot chocolate while it was eighty-eight degrees outside.

"It's good to see you again, Mary," Mrs. Hunter said to Tater's mom. "How are you these days?"

I kept looking around the room for any evidence Fox was there. The walls were covered with hundreds of pictures of Tater from when he was a baby all the way until now. His mom must have thought he was the greatest kid in the world.

She rocked back and forth in an old wooden chair. Her eyes stared straight ahead. I suspected she was blind. She had fluffy pink hair that was oily and looked like it hadn't been washed in weeks. "No one comes to see me anymore," she complained. "No one cares."

"Maybe it's because her son is a lunatic," Dana whispered to me.

Tater's mom stopped rocking. "Who are the children? I love children."

Mr. Hunter shrugged and motioned for me to say something. Melissa nodded like it was my job to explain who we were and why we were there. I'm not proud of what I said. "We're friends of Tater."

Dana almost choked to death.

Tater's mom smiled and started rocking again. "He loves animals and children. He'll be happy to see you."

Not if I could help it. I had to get out of that room and search the house for Fox or some clue as to where he was. I hated to be that close to the answer but feel trapped in my seat. I asked the one question that would get me out of there. "Where's your bathroom?"

"It's down the hall, honey," she said. "Second door on your right."

I didn't waste any time and headed for the hall. I waved for Melissa and Dana to follow me. They jumped up and followed without any argument. We were covered in sweat from the fireplace, so it was a relief to get out of there.

"Keep your eyes open," I told them. "We've got to find Fox." We opened the doors to every room and peeked inside. Nothing appeared unusual until we reached the last room with a sign on the door that looked like a kid made it.

I almost had a heart attack when I pried the door open. There were stuffed animals everywhere! A bear, lion, possum, squirrel, duck, beaver, rabbit, wolf—every animal you can think of. My heart wouldn't stop racing. With every step I took I was afraid I'd find Fox stuffed like one of those poor animals.

"Looking for something?" a man's voice said from behind us. Dana and Melissa shrieked. It was Tater the Exterminator! He closed the door and shook a finger at us. "You shouldn't be here." I didn't know what he planned to do with us, but I knew we were trapped in the room with a crazy man.

The girls held on to me. "Do something, Joe," Melissa pleaded.

Tater rolled his sleeves up. "I haven't decided if I should call the police or stuff you like one of these animals." He rubbed his chin like he was struggling with the decision. "The three of you would look good stuffed by the curtains," he said, pointing to the only window in the room.

Dana stepped away from me and towards him. I tried to stop her. "That's enough!" she shouted at him. "Quit being a big meanie!"

He stared at her for a moment then let his shoulders slump. "I'm sorry. I'm not good with people."

"You need to be nicer," Melissa added. "People will like you better."

I didn't know what to say. Dana and Melissa had

expected me to protect them, but I failed. They stood up for themselves and saved all of us. How was I supposed to be able to protect Fox?

"I remember you," Tater said, pointing at me. "You're the kid with the fox."

"Not anymore," I reminded him. "You took him away from me. Where is he? You're going to take us to him right now."

He shook his head. "I can't do that. It's too late."

I stopped breathing. My worst nightmare was confirmed. There was no way to save Fox. He was gone forever. It was my fault. I had failed to protect him.

"Joe," Melissa said, grabbing my arm, "you've got to see this."

My stomach churned. I was afraid she had found Fox stuffed like the other animals. She led me to a small metal table with papers and pictures on it. But one piece of paper stood out from all the others.

It was a flier, like the ones posted on the walls at school. Only this one wasn't about a dance, party, or fundraiser. Fox's picture was on the flier.

THE TALKING FOX was printed above the picture. It went on to explain Fox would be at the Grand Vulpine Hotel in Las Vegas giving a live performance that night at 8 p.m.

"I'm sorry," Tater repeated. "Mr. Connors paid me ten thousand dollars to capture the fox." He looked at Dana like he had to explain himself to her. "I needed the money to help my mom keep this house. I didn't mean to hurt anyone." He seemed truly sorry. And I knew a thing or two about trying to save a house.

Tater pointed to his ears and complained, "Everyone makes fun of me. I have huge ears that look like potatoes." I was confused. His ears looked normal to me but his hotdog nose was the right size for a hotdog bun. I wondered if any of us see ourselves the way we truly are.

"That's how I got the name Tater." He shook his head and sighed. "I don't want to be a mean person. I just want people to like me."

I wondered if that was why Shane had grown three times meaner. I had embarrassed him with that homework assignment I wrote for him. Everyone made fun of him for the first time in his life, and his reputation was never the same.

"We've got to stop them," Melissa said. She was talking about Mr. Connors and Shane. "They're going to exploit Fox."

I hoped Mr. and Mrs. Hunter were ready to leave. "We need to get out of here. I've got to talk to my mom." We were running out of time and I had to explain all of this to her. We had to find a way to get to Las Vegas and save Fox.

LATER SUNDAY

I jumped out of Mr. and Mrs. Hunter's car when we got to my house and ran to the front door screaming, "Mom! Mom!" The door swung open and her eyes bugged out of her head like she thought I was being chased by an alligator.

I couldn't breathe when I reached her, so I handed her the flier I brought back. She didn't say anything for a minute; then she stared at me and asked, "Is this a joke?"

"It's not a joke," Melissa confirmed as she joined me with Dana by her side. "We got it from Tater the Exterminator."

My mom's hair turned gray right then and there. "You did what?"

"He's a nice guy," Dana added. "He's just misunderstood because he has potato ears."

My mom looked more confused than ever. She took a deep breath and tried to process what we told her. "Let me see if I understand this correctly…"

I knew right away we were in big trouble.

"You kids somehow met with Tater the Exterminator—when you clearly told me the Hunters were taking you out to eat?" Her face was turning red.

"We had hot chocolate around a nice fire," Dana said defensively.

We all jumped when Mr. Hunter honked his horn from the driveway. He and his wife waved at us like they just had the best time of their lives. They drove out of our driveway and into theirs across the street. I wanted to be in the car with them. I wasn't sure it was safe around my mom.

She glanced at the flier again and sighed. "Everyone inside," she ordered. "We've got a lot to figure out."

My uncle was sitting on the couch, watching wrestling again. I laughed when I pictured Fox there the day before flexing his puny arms and calling himself Mr. Awesome Muscles. I missed the little guy. "Everything okay?" my uncle asked, not paying attention to us.

My mom handed him the flier. He glanced at it then set it down on the couch next to him. We all thought it was odd he didn't care while the wrestling match was still on. But then he jumped up, grabbed the flier again like he just realized what it said, and shouted, "What the heck?"

"This is not what Fox wants," I said to all of them. "He's scared and alone."

My mom stared at my uncle in a way I'd only seen them do a few times. They had some type of secret communication between them that no one else could decipher. They developed it growing up as brother and sister. I wished I had the power to read people's minds.

My uncle nodded and said, "Las Vegas, huh? We need a plane and I've got a friend who owes me a favor." He winked at me. "Let me go make a call." He disappeared into the kitchen.

My mom took his place on the couch and patted the cushions for all of us to take a seat next to her. She laughed and couldn't stop. "This is not the weekend I had planned." We laughed with her. Everything was different with Fox in our lives. But everything was better.

"I hope he's okay," Dana said when the laughter died down. Her voice was sadder than I'd ever heard it.

Melissa wrapped an arm around her. "He will be. Joe will make sure of it." She smiled at me and it made me feel woozy. You would think the saying 'butterflies in your stomach' meant you felt awesome like you were flying. Nope! It felt more like I was trying to fly but instead doing a belly flop on the kitchen floor.

"Okay," my uncle said, standing in front of us now. "The good news is my friend can fly us to Vegas and get us there before the show starts. The bad news is he can only take two of us." He studied all of us on the couch. "Who's it gonna be?"

Everyone looked at me like it was my decision. I had to go because I couldn't let my best friend down. While everyone in that room wanted to help Fox, there was only one other person who loved him as much as me. "It looks like we're going to Vegas, Mom."

"Alright," my uncle agreed. "It's settled. My friend will meet you at the airport in twenty minutes. You need to leave now if you're going to make it in time." He shoved us out the door.

"Wait," my mom said to him. "What's your friend's name?"

I swear my uncle chuckled. "You'll know him

when you get there. And don't worry about anything. Me and Dana will take Melissa home and we'll lock up here."

He stopped me before I got to the driveway. "Bring him home, Joe. Whatever you have to do, bring Fox home."

The airport was extra windy when we got there. And my uncle was right. We knew his friend.

"Hope you didn't eat any of those eggs," Mr. Jim Bob joked. I wondered how that straw hat stayed on top of his head. Maybe it was glued. "They don't taste any good coming up a second time." He had plenty of experience with that after eating Old Nelly's rotten eggs.

"How safe is this plane?" my mom asked, knocking on it. The plane looked like it was made of plastic and weighed less than me. Okay, that's an exaggeration, but it didn't look like any plane I'd ever seen on TV. It was much smaller and there was a good chance it would tip over if the wind blew hard enough.

"This plane is safer than safe," Mr. Bob assured her. "I've been flying her for thirty-five years, and she's only crashed thirty-four times!" My mom didn't laugh. "C'mon now," he pleaded. "It's a pilot's joke. It's funny."

My mom grabbed my shoulders and made sure she had my full attention. "This is not going to work. We'll find another way."

We had less than six hours to get to Las Vegas. This was our best chance of making that happen. "We can't give up on Fox. He's part of our family."

She cracked her neck and rolled her shoulders back. "Let's do this."

Five minutes later, we were on the plane, riding down the runway, waiting for it to take off. The end of the runway was coming up fast, and we were still on the ground driving at a million miles an hour. I tasted my hot chocolate a second time that day. My mom shrieked.

Mr. Bob laughed hysterically when we took off at the last second. He shot the plane straight up into the air like a rocket. "Going up high to touch the sky! Yeeeeeeehaw!"

SUNDAY NIGHT

Four hours later, I was standing in front of the Grand Vulpine Hotel in Las Vegas with my mom. Well, not exactly in front of it. More like half a mile away because the line to get inside went on forever.

The hotel was like a mirrored tower. It was dark outside so I couldn't see myself in it, but I saw the one thing that took my breath away. It was a huge image of Fox lit up in lights along the front of the hotel. The lights flashed on for a minute to show my best friend then they flashed off. Every time they came back on I was amazed at how spectacular it looked.

"I hope we get inside," said the lady in front of us. "This is the hottest show of the year."

The big guy with her shrugged his shoulders. His hair was spiked and he had a tattoo of a spider on his cheek. "If we don't, then we don't. There's another ventriloquist across the street."

I asked my mom what a ventriloquist was. She said it was a person who made things that can't speak look like they were talking. It was like magic. This was good news. I wondered if everyone else thought Fox was controlled by a ventriloquist.

My mom glanced at her watch and said what I was thinking. "We can't just stand out here. We may never get inside." She pulled me out of the line and we walked around everyone like we were just passing by. There were young people and old people but no kids. Tall people and short people. White people, black people, Hispanics, Orientals. The whole world had come to see Fox.

A huge man covered with muscles was walking toward us. His muscles were so huge that his tank top barely fit across his chest. He was bigger than Mr. Awesome Muscles! He stopped every few steps and said something to the people in line. I heard what it was when we got closer to him. It was the one thing I didn't want to hear.

"Show's sold out," he barked. "Everyone go home."

My heart sank. My best friend was trapped inside the building in front of us. I don't want to sound weird, but I could feel how scared he was. He was just a kid who wanted to go home.

My mom marched right up to the muscle man and said, "We need to get inside. We've got a friend trapped in there."

He shook his head. "I couldn't let you in—even if your name was Donald Trump. There's not a seat left in the house." He stepped around us like we were invisible and kept telling people to go home.

I felt like crying but I refused to do it. I marched behind the big muscle man and tugged on his tank top. He seemed as tall as the hotel when he turned and faced me.

"What?" he barked.

"Please," I begged him. "We've got to help Fox."

He rubbed his eyebrows like he had a headache. "Sorry, kid. Even if every seat was empty I still couldn't let you in. You have to be at least twenty-one and have a picture ID." He squinted his eyes. "You don't look twenty-one to me." He started to laugh but stopped when I stared into his eyes.

"It's you," he said, his expression softening. "You're the kid in the video, the one who talks to the fox. What are you doing out here?" He motioned for me and my mom to follow him to the hotel. "We've got to get you on stage. This is your big night."

We weaved through hundreds or thousands of people to get to the back stage entrance. "Out of the way!" the muscle man kept shouting at everyone in front of us. "Superstar coming through!"

It seemed like hours before we were waiting in the wings to see Fox on stage. I peered through the curtains and saw the audience staring back. Some people were standing and some were sitting. There were more people than I'd ever seen in my entire life. I wondered how long was left until Fox was on stage and if we had time to stop it before it happened.

"Ladies and gentlemen," someone announced over the

speakers above and around us. "Welcome to the Grand Vulpine Hotel and the hottest show on Earth. Here he is—the talking fox!"

The crowd went wild with cheers, whistles, and claps. I started to rush on stage and stop this, but another big guy stepped in front of me and blocked me. "We need you up front," he said to the muscle man next to me. "There's a fight." They both rushed away without saying anything to me.

When I looked back at the stage, I saw Mr. Connors pulling Fox on a leash to the center. Fox was thrashing all around, trying to break free. I wanted to run out there, grab Fox, and fly right back to Alabama, but my mom stopped me.

"Not yet, Jonah," she said. "If we do anything rash, they're going to kick us out of here." I hated that she was right.

"So, Fox," Mr. Connors said into a microphone. "How do you like Las Vegas?" That was an odd question. Maybe Mr. Connors and Shane had practiced a whole routine with Fox, but I doubted Fox agreed to any of it.

Fox didn't respond and lay down on the floor. He was shivering. A lot of people from the audience booed.

Mr. Connors yanked on the leash. Fox had to be choking. "I said, how do you like Las Vegas?"

Fox still wouldn't say anything.

My heart raced when Shane marched onto the stage from the other side. He walked right up to Fox and kicked him in the side! Fox yelped in a cry of pain that shattered my heart.

"Leave him alone!" someone shouted. The boos from the crowd got louder and louder.

That was enough. I couldn't stand by anymore. My mom nodded approval. Right before I set foot on stage, someone else grabbed my shoulders and stopped me. Really? Now?

I turned and saw the one face I didn't expect to see. It was Tater the Exterminator! He was toting a huge plastic bag over his back.

"Get your hands off my son," my mom growled.

He set the bag down and put his hands in the air. His hotdog nose stuck out like a sore thumb.

"Why are you here?" I asked him. If he had never come into our yard and our house, Fox wouldn't have been on that stage. He was just as guilty as Mr. Connors and Shane.

He put his hands down and sighed. "I made a mistake. I came to fix it." He looked back and forth from me to my mom. "You've got to let me go out there and make this right."

I was about to tell him no because it was my responsibility, but my mom put a hand on my shoulder. "Go on then," she told Tater.

He grabbed the huge bag from the floor and nodded. "Thank you." He brushed past me and right onto the stage.

"Stop!" Tater shouted at Mr. Connors and Shane. They both glared at him. "I came to return this." He opened his bag and dumped its contents on the floor. It looked like a lot of money. I guessed it was the ten thousand dollars Mr. Connors had paid him to capture Fox.

Mr. Connors handed the leash to his son and walked over to Tater. "You fool. Do you think you're better than me? You'll never be anything more than a freak with potato ears." He faced the crowd and laughed. No one laughed with him. He returned his attention to Tater. "This is my world. There's nothing you can do about it."

Tater took a deep breath and looked back at me. I figured he was going to walk away and say he was sorry. I didn't know why any of us thought we could stop this. "I may not be able to do anything," he admitted, "but these guys can." He pointed to someone behind me.

Two cops passed me and marched onto the stage. "Charles Connors and Shane Connors," one cop said, "you're under arrest for kidnapping and animal cruelty." They slapped cuffs on both of them. "You have the right to remain silent," the second cop said.

Mr. Connors wouldn't stop laughing. He spit on Tater when the cop ushered him toward the stage exit. "You're going down with me!" he shouted. "You'll pay for this!"

"Maybe," Tater said, "but at least I tried to make things right."

I rushed onto the stage to get Fox. I couldn't wait any longer. My friend was scared and hurt. He had to know I was there for him. I kneeled next to him on the floor, unhooked the leash, and hugged him. He hugged me back.

"I knew you'd come for me," he whispered, smiling. He didn't want the audience to hear him.

I stood back up. "Was there ever any doubt?" He shook his head. "Let's go home, Fox."

My mom was talking to Tater when we joined her. "Why did you help us?"

He looked at Fox and smiled. "I forgot who I was. I forgot why I got into this business in the first place." He gazed into the crowd. "I love animals."

It was at that moment I realized they could hear everything we said. The crowd cheered for Tater and clapped. He had a huge smile on his face.

"I'm glad you're okay," I said to Fox. "Let's get you out of here."

"Wait," Fox whispered to me. I bent down close to

him so I could hear. "There's something I want to say to them." His eyes were pleading like it was something important that would change the world.

I wasn't sure if it was a good idea or not. Everyone already knew he could talk. Now he could say whatever he wanted and not what someone was trying to force him to say. If he was brave enough to say something in front of thousands of people, I wouldn't be the one to stop him.

Fox walked back to the center of the stage on four paws. He faced the crowd. They gasped when he stood up on his two hind legs. He looked at me one last time and winked. Whatever he was going to say would be life changing.

The crowd was silent, waiting for his words.

That's when he shouted the one thing no one expected.

"I love Las Vegas!"

The crowd went crazy and chanted his name. "Fox! Fox! Fox! Fox! Fox! Fox! Fox! Fox! Fox! Fox! Fox! Fox! Fox! Fox! Fox! Fox!"

It had to be the greatest moment of Fox's life. I was so proud of him. Everything was exactly the way it was always meant to be.

I never expected it all to fall apart.

MONDAY MORNING

We got home early that morning. Like six o'clock in the morning early, thanks to Mr. Jim Bob's plane. My mom had suggested we get a hotel room in Las Vegas for the night, but I wanted to get Fox home so he could be comfortable in the den I made for him. And I had those bad memories about the last time we were in a hotel room.

My uncle Mike and Dana met us at the airport. Dana was so happy to see Fox that she ran up and tackled him. My uncle high fived Fox and flexed muscles with him.

We were all wide awake so we agreed to go back to my house to get something to eat and catch up with Fox. It was like a family reunion and no one would stop talking. You would think we hadn't seen Fox in years.

My mom wouldn't let me out of the car when we pulled into our driveway. Uncle Mike and Dana were behind us in their car. She rolled her window down and motioned for my uncle to come to ours.

"What's wrong?" he asked, standing by her window.

She pointed to the house. "I thought you said you were going to lock up." I looked at the front door. It was wide open.

"I did," he replied. He motioned for Dana to get out of their car and into ours. "Roll your window up and lock the doors. I'll find out why the front door's open."

My mom tried to stop him. "Wait," she begged. "We should call the police."

He glanced into the back seat where Fox was asleep with his tongue out. Even after all we had done to save Fox, it was still illegal to keep him. "No, we shouldn't." He walked past the car and into the house.

A lot of time had passed, and my uncle didn't come back out. My mom was crying. I feared something bad had happened to him. All of this was my fault—everything that happened over the weekend. If I had just written Shane's homework the way he wanted me to, none of this would ever have happened.

I opened my car door and raced to the house.

"Jonah!" my mom shouted.

I wasn't prepared for what I found when I stepped inside.

Everything was turned over and broken. The TV was smashed. The couches were ripped apart. The pictures were shattered.

My mom rushed in after me. "Don't ever do that again! You almost gave me a…" She didn't say anything else when she saw the damage.

We both jumped when my uncle came out of the kitchen. "I don't understand," he said. "They didn't take anything."

We all turned when Dana and Fox joined us. And that's when we saw it. Painted in big red letters above the doorway were the words GIVE US THE FOX.

I had thought all of this was over. But it looked like there would always be people looking for Fox. Like my mom said, good people and bad people. Mr. Connors and Shane were only the beginning.

"This is about me, isn't it?" Fox asked. He couldn't read but he was good at figuring things out. He looked through the trashed house. "All of this is because of me."

None of us could deny it, but no one wanted to admit it.

"Look," Fox said, "it's not safe for any of you if I'm here." He nodded his head at me like I didn't have any choice but to accept what he said. "I've got to disappear. They'll never stop looking for me."

"You can't go," Dana cried.

My uncle threw his hands up like he hated the idea but couldn't think of any other options. "Whoever these people are, they're going to come back." My mom reminded him that if the police were involved then Fox would be taken away for good. There was no upside. There was no way to win.

Her eyes sparkled. She held up a finger like she did whenever she had a good idea.

She stared at my uncle again in the way they secretly communicated. Why couldn't I read their minds? I hated being left out of a conversation that didn't even exist. I had a feeling they were discussing Fox's future. All I knew was I didn't want him to leave.

"I don't like it," my uncle finally said, "but everyone get into my car."

I wondered if we were going back to Las Vegas or running away. I didn't want to do either. This was my home and the one place I could guard my best friend. "What's going on?"

My mom motioned for me, Dana, and Fox to move toward the door. "I know someone who can help us."

Fox tapped her on the leg. "Mr. Awesome Muscles?"

She chuckled and said, "No, Fox. Not Mr. Awesome Muscles." She redirected her attention to me. "Do you remember how to get to Tater's house?"

Of course I remembered. He lived with his mom on Brown Street in the big orange house. I couldn't think of any reason to go there unless we wanted to roast marshmallows over their burning hot fireplace. "Yeah … why?"

My mom tried to close the front door after we were all out of the house, but the knob was busted.

She sighed and followed my uncle to his car. "Tater may be the only person who can help Fox now."

MONDAY AFTERNOON

We sat around Tater's living room with his mom for hours. He hadn't returned from Las Vegas yet. Even though we sweated from the hot fireplace, his mom asked for a blanket to keep her warm. Her eyes didn't move.

"He's a good boy," she assured us about Tater. "He'd never hurt anyone." She rocked back and forth in her chair, nodding her head and smiling as my mom placed a blanket on her. "Thank you, honey."

I doubted Tater wouldn't hurt anyone. He killed bugs and captured animals for a living. And what about those stuffed animals in his room? It was like he collected them for trophies.

Fox waved his paws at me then rubbed his belly. "I'm starving. Do they have any chicken here?"

Tater's mom stopped rocking. "We only eat fruits and vegetables. You can have all the broccoli you want."

Dana stuck her tongue out and acted like she had to vomit. "I vote we get some fast food as soon as we leave."

Fox agreed with her. "We don't want slow food. We want fast food."

The front door opened, and Tater the Exterminator stepped in. He had on the same clothes as the night before.

Fox's whole body was shaking.

"Hey, Mama," Tater said as he closed the door and joined us. "Hey, everyone else. What are you doing here?"

"Christopher Joseph Allen," his mom said, standing up now. "Where have you been all night? I've been worried sick."

He rushed over to her. "It's okay, Mama. Sit back down." He looked around the room at all of us. My uncle stood like a statue with his chest out. He was ready to protect us if Tater tried to hurt anyone.

Tater faced me and Dana. "Shouldn't you kids be in school?" Making sure Fox was safe was more important. And I can't lie—I was afraid to go back to school. I had no idea if Shane would be there or not. I wanted to see Melissa and tell her what happened, but that would have to wait.

"What's going to happen to Shane and his dad?" I asked him. I figured he knew the answer because he was the one who made sure they were taken away.

He put his hands in his pockets and shrugged. "It's up to the courts. For animal cruelty, they could be fined six thousand dollars and go to prison for a year." Mr. Connors had plenty of money. He had given Tater ten thousand dollars just to capture Fox. I wondered what happened to the money Tater dumped on the stage and left behind. If I was lucky, Shane would go away for a year.

He looked at Fox's body shaking next to mine. "It's okay," Tater promised him. "I'm not going to hurt you."

Fox calmed down a little, but Dana wanted answers. "What about all those animals in your room? You hurt them. All of them!"

Tater shook his head. "I bought those years ago on the internet. They remind me why I do what I do." He smiled at Dana. "I do everything I can to save them."

I was confused. I thought for sure Tater was a

bad person who hurt animals. Sure, he was crazy. But maybe I had misunderstood him the whole time. After all, he did help us get Fox back.

"I was right about you," my mom said. She stood by his side. "We need your help."

Tater took his hands out of his pockets and laughed. "I'm not sure I can help anyone. I shouldn't have given that money back."

His mom stopped rocking again and said, "It was the right thing to do. We'll find another way."

My mom looked at both of them like she had no idea what they were talking about. I explained it to her. "They're going to lose the house. They needed that money."

Tater hung his head and scratched it. "Life is funny when you try to do the right thing. I can't win."

My mom cleared her throat and nodded at my uncle. I wasn't sure if they were talking to each other in their heads or not. "How much money do you need?"

"To stay here?" Tater asked. "About five thousand dollars. But that's not going to happen." He looked like he was about to cry. "Don't worry about us. We'll make it. We always do."

My mom took a deep breath and stared at Fox. He wasn't shaking anymore. "How much would it cost for you to do pest control at my house?" she asked Tater. "I hate ants and roaches."

He shrugged. "Your house is pretty big. I could do it for forty dollars a month."

My mom grabbed her purse off the floor. She pulled out her checkbook and wrote a check then handed it to Tater.

He looked it and whistled. "I can't take this," he said, handing it back to her. "It's for four thousand and eight hundred dollars. I don't accept charity anymore." His mom nodded her agreement.

My mom wouldn't take the check back. "It's not charity. You said you could provide my house with pest control for forty dollars a month."

He nodded. "Yes ma'am. But even if you prepaid me for a year, that would only be four hundred and eighty dollars for all twelve months."

She pushed his hand with the check back towards him. "We're going to be living in that house for a very long time, Christopher. I've prepaid you for ten years." His mom smiled wide. "And you have a beautiful name. You should use it."

Tater—I mean Christopher—was speechless for the first time. He finally said, "There's no way I can thank you enough for this."

Dana jumped up from her seat. "You can start by getting some real food for us."

Fox nodded vigorously. "Fast food. Not slow food."

My mom held her hands out. "Just a minute. Christopher, we came here because we need your help. Fox is in danger and we have to find a safe place for him."

He stuffed the check into his pocket and nodded. "There's a wildlife sanctuary about thirty minutes from here." He looked at Fox. "I've taken foxes there before."

My mom looked at me and nodded. "Then that's where we're going. We'll get some fast food on the way."

Fox jumped off the couch and stood on his hind legs in front of my mom. "Chicken is fast. Broccoli is slow."

MONDAY EVENING

I felt sick when we arrived at the wildlife sanctuary. It was a huge place with acres of land and buildings for sick, injured, or orphaned animals. Christopher said he had brought all sorts of animals here for help, from skunks to bears. It was the right place for Fox, but I didn't want to let him go.

"Got another orphan, Christopher?" a lady in white shorts and a red T-shirt asked when we arrived. She had a pair of latex gloves on.

"Yep," he replied. "This one's special."

"They're all special," she said. "Let me have a look." She bent down and inspected Fox's hairy body. He was standing on all four paws in an attempt to blend in. She laid him down so she could check everything. The lady froze when she looked into his eyes. "His eyes are bright blue. I've never seen anything like this." She was about to see and hear a lot more things she'd never seen or heard before.

"Foxes are known carriers of rabies," she told all of us as she stood back up. "Have any of you been bitten or scratched?"

We all shook our heads. I didn't know what rabies were, but Fox never even had a cold.

"Okay then," she said. "We'll take him."

My heart dropped. There was a huge part of me that hoped they wouldn't take Fox. I wasn't sure when I could see him again. Christopher said visitors were only allowed in the afternoons when I was at school and on Saturdays when I worked with my mom at the farmers' market.

"I'd like to make a donation," my mom said. She pulled out her checkbook and wrote another check. The lady's eyes looked like they were going to pop out of her head when she saw how much money it was.

"Fox is different from other animals," my mom continued, nodding her head slowly to make sure the lady paid attention to every word. "His favorite food is chicken. He likes to sleep in a tent or den. And he loves to watch wrestling."

The lady raised her eyebrows.

"Exactly how much money was under my lumpy mattress?" I asked my mom. We had found enough money under my mattress to save our house months ago. I wondered how much was left over.

"There was enough, Jonah," was all she would say.

I tried to be happy for Fox because he had a chance to be with his own kind. He was lost without his parents and nothing would ever make up for that. But maybe this place would help him.

The lady stepped away to talk to Christopher. "Don't leave me here," Fox begged me. "I don't want to do this. I'm scared."

Dana ran over to Fox and hugged him. "I'll never forget you." She kissed the top of his head and went back to my uncle, crying.

My heart was being ripped to pieces. I wanted to grab my best friend and run away with him. I was leaving him behind in a world he wasn't familiar with. Were we doing the right thing? I didn't want to say goodbye. I was completely numb. How was I supposed to live my life not knowing how Fox was? How was I supposed to live without him?

"Maybe it'll be okay," Fox said, rubbing his side against my leg. "They don't serve chicken pot pie here, but I'll survive." He smiled and looked up at me with his bright blue eyes.

He was trying to make me feel better. He was the one whose world was being taken away from him, but he wanted to make sure I was okay. He had caused more trouble than anyone else in my life. And he was the best thing that ever happened to me.

He held out his arm with the bracelet. I held out mine. "Best friends," we said together. I tried not to cry. Fox stood up on his hind legs and hugged me. I never wanted to let him go. Mr. Awesome Muscles.

"He'll do well with the other two foxes," the lady said when she returned with Christopher. I could see the foxes partially hidden in the tall grass in the field across from us. They were bigger and older than Fox. "They've come a long ways since you brought them to us a few months ago."

Christopher nodded like he was impressed. "You did a good job. I wasn't sure they'd make it."

She smiled. "It's what we do. They were in bad shape after those hunters shot them." She paused and shook her head. "It still amazes me. They got away somehow and refused to die. It's like those foxes were fighting for something. Or someone."

Fox turned away from me and looked towards the other foxes. Then he said the two words I never thought I'd hear him say.

"Mom? Dad?"

He raced off toward them without looking back and leaped over the fence. The older foxes ran together toward Fox at the same time. Fox shouted their names over and over. "Mom! Dad! Mom! Dad!"

Fox had always believed he would find them. My heart was going to explode.

Fox and his parents jumped all around each other. They rubbed their sides together and licked each other's faces. Fox finally had everything he was looking for. Seeing them so happy made me miss my dad at that moment.

My mom hugged me from behind. "I'm here for you, Jonah. Mom's here."

"I miss Dad," I confided in her.

She held me tighter. "Your father loved you very much. And he would be proud of the man you're becoming. He'll always be with us. I can see him in you."

I took a few deep breaths and cleared my throat. "You're the best mom ever."

"I know," she said. "That's what it says on my mug at home." We both laughed.

The lady with the red shirt stepped up to us and handed me a shirt exactly like hers. "This is the only one I have. I'll order some more in your size."

I didn't understand. "What is this?"

My mom smiled. "It's for your after-school job. Uncle Mike will bring you here and I'll take you home after work."

My head spun for a moment. Did I hear that right? I could come here to see Fox after school every day? No way!

I ran to the fence Fox had leaped over and shouted his name. "Fox!" It sounded odd because they were all foxes, but only mine could talk. "I'm not leaving you here alone! I'm coming back tomorrow! I got a job here!"

He ran back to the fence with his parents. He grinned and wagged his tail when they reached me. "Guess you're stuck with me."

I grinned back. "I guess so. Nothing can keep us apart."

His mom and dad stood on all four paws on each side of him and looked up at me from the other side of the fence. They were tall and majestic. I could tell right away they couldn't talk or move like him. They sniffed my pants and licked my hands through slits in the fence. It tickled.

Fox leaped back over the fence and stood next to me with a serious look on his face. "You know what we should do? We should go to China."

I couldn't keep a straight face. I remembered when we first met and he convinced me it was possible to dig a hole to China. And when he came back a few days ago and we laughed about it. I don't know how I ever lived without Fox. "You're my best friend and the brother I never had."

"You welcomed me into your family," Fox said. "Now I welcome you into mine." I couldn't stop smiling.

My mom yelled my name. She was with my uncle, Dana, and my new boss at a table they set up outside. "We have cake!" she yelled. "Let's celebrate!"

"Cake?" Fox asked, licking his lips. "I want cake."

I remembered the last time Fox had cake. It had given him that nasty fart that smelled like tuna and broccoli and onions and vinegar and dirty feet and dirty underwear all mixed together.

I threw out my hands and shouted, "No!" I love Fox, but every kid has his limits.

Fox has gotten sick, and I've got to do everything I can to help him get better. We'll meet an American Indian who tells us how Fox can walk and talk. But we also meet a man from another country who wants to take Fox away.

My Fox Ate My Alarm Clock is entertaining for kids of all ages, and adults who secretly never grew up.

AVAILABLE AT AMAZON.COM
Print and Ebook

DAVID BLAZE

This series includes:

1. My Fox Ate My Homework
2. My Fox Ate My Cake
3. My Fox Ate My Alarm Clock
4. My Cat Ate My Homework
5. My Fox Begins
6. My Fox Ate My Report Card

You can keep up with everything I'm doing at:

www.davidblazebooks.com

Be sure to click the Follow button next my name (David Blaze) on Amazon.com to be notified when my new books are released.

And you can follow me on Facebook. Just search for David Blaze, Children's Author. Be sure to like the page!

If you enjoyed my story, please tell your friends and family. I'd also appreciate it if you'd leave a review on Amazon.com and tell me what you think about my best friend, Fox.

See you soon!